YOU'RE NICKED,
Ms Wiz

Other books about Ms Wiz

TERENCE BLACKER
YOU'RE NICKED,
Ms Wiz

Illustrated by
TONY ROSS

ANDERSEN PRESS
LONDON

This edition first published in 2010 by
ANDERSEN PRESS LIMITED
20 Vauxhall Bridge Road
London SW1V 2SA
www.andersenpress.co.uk

First published by Piccadilly Press Limited in 1989

British Library Cataloguing in Publication Data available.

ISBN 978 1 84939 151 1

Printed in China

CHAPTER ONE
A SORT OF MISSING PERSON

"Daydreaming *again*, Lizzie Thompson?"

The words came to Lizzie from far away. She had been staring out of the window into the playground at St Barnabas School, unaware that her class teacher Mr Bailey was standing in front of her desk.

"Sorry, sir," she said quietly. "I was thinking about my cat."

"Your what?"

"My cat. Waif."

"Oh I see," said Mr Bailey. "Here we all are in the middle of an English lesson, discussing similes, and Lizzie's off in a private fantasy about her cat. That's absolutely fine then, isn't it?"

"It's lost, sir," said Jack, who was one of Lizzie's best friends. "It disappeared yesterday."

"Well, staring out of the window's not going to help, is it?" said the teacher briskly.

"Cruel," muttered Podge at the back of the class. "How would he like it?"

Mr Bailey thumped Lizzie's desk. "I would like it if Class Five did some *work* for a change," he said loudly. "Now, back to similes. Here is an example of a simile: 'Podge sits at his desk like a sack of potatoes.' Now who can give me another simile?"

Caroline put up her hand.

"Our teacher is like someone who doesn't know how you feel when you lose a pet and then he can't even manage to be nice when a person's so upset that she can't concentrate on a boring English lesson, especially when it's taught by a cat-hater. Or is that a metaphor, sir?"

Everybody in Class Five laughed – except for Lizzie, who was looking out of the window again.

After school, Lizzie ran home, hoping for the best but fearing the worst. All day, she had been unable to think of anything but Waif. Now, as she ran, she remembered the winter's day when she had found him, cold, shivering and hungry, among the dustbins by her house. He had hardly been more than a kitten. When no one came to feed him after a few days, she took him in. "Waif" she had called him.

And now he was gone.

"I've looked everywhere," said Lizzie's mother, when she arrived home. "In cupboards. Down the street. In the park—" she hesitated. "Under cars."

Tears welled up in Lizzie's eyes.

"You think he's dead, don't you?" she said.

Mrs Thompson put her arm around her daughter. "It's dangerous for cats around here. People drive so fast," she said, adding gently, "He's had a good innings."

"He's only six, Mummy," sobbed Lizzie. "Since when has six been a good innings?"

She ran upstairs to her room and slammed the door.

The next morning, Lizzie did something she had never done before. After waving goodbye to her mother at the end of her street, she walked towards St Barnabas as usual but, instead of turning right towards the High Street where she normally met Jack and Caroline, she turned left into the park.

"I just know that Waif is alive," she muttered to herself, "and today I'm going to find him."

"Good for you, dear," said an old tramp woman who was sitting on a park bench nearby, but Lizzie was too deep in thought to pay her any attention.

Lizzie's plan to find Waif went like this:

1. Look under a lot of bushes.
2. Pin up on trees the notices she had written late last night. They read: "LOST: BEAUTIFUL WHITE CAT WITH GINGER PATCHES (MALE). ANSWERS TO NAME OF WAIF (OR WAIFY). MUCH LOVED. IF FOUND, PLEASE PHONE 579 8282."

3. Go to the police station and ask for their help.

But nothing went right. All morning, Lizzie looked under bushes without success. She pinned up her notices, but then there were so many other lost cat notices that she began to despair.

"Everyone round here seems to have lost a cat recently," she sighed.

Finally, late that afternoon, she stumbled into the local police station.

"And what can I do for you, young lady?" asked the police constable behind the desk.

"I've lost my cat," said Lizzie nervously.

The policeman chuckled, as if he'd just been told a rather good joke.

"D'you know what this is, young lady?" he said, tapping a big book in front of him. "It's called the Crime

Book. In this book, I note down all the really terrible things that people get up to in this area. Theft, hit-and-run, breaking and entering, bag-snatching, vagrancy, motor offences, missing persons, grievous bodily harm – all sorts of nastiness."

"I see," said Lizzie.

"And now you want me to add to the list of ongoing, unsolved misdemeanours one little moggie that's gone walkabout, right?"

"He's a sort of missing person, too."

"Listen, miss. I know cats. They wander. Especially toms."

"He's not a tom," said Lizzie. "He's . . . neuter."

The policeman looked confused. "New to what?" he asked. "If he's new to the area, no wonder he's lost."

"PC Boote." Another policeman,

who had overheard the conversation,
now joined them. He winked at
Lizzie. "When the young lady says
her cat's neuter, I think she means
that he's—" He whispered into the
police constable's ear.

"Oh dear, oh dear," said PC Boote,
wincing slightly. He turned to Lizzie.
"When did this, er, neutering happen
then?"

"Don't worry, miss," said the

second policeman quickly. "We'll let you know if we hear of a lost cat. Just give PC Boote here the details."

Sighing heavily, PC Boote noted in the Crime Book Lizzie's name, telephone number and her description of Waif.

"Looking for lost cats," he muttered. "I've heard it all now."

Lizzie turned to leave. Somehow finding Waif was turning out to be even more difficult than she thought it was going to be.

Miserably, she stood on the steps of the police station, wondering what to do next.

"What you need is a spot of magic," said a familiar voice. It was the tramp who had seen Lizzie in the park. She was pushing a pram full of old rags, on which sat a china cat with odd, glowing eyes.

"Thanks," sniffed Lizzie. "And

where exactly do you find magic these days?"

"Follow me," said the tramp.

CHAPTER TWO
A STRANGE COINCIDENCE

Mr Bailey was panicking.

Yesterday, Lizzie Thompson had been upset about her cat. And what had he done? He had shouted, told her to get on with her work and hit the desk with his hand. And now Lizzie was absent from class. He had gone too far yet again. He would just have to ask the head teacher to ring her mother.

Mrs Thompson was panicking.

When the head teacher had rung to find out whether Lizzie was ill, she had been at work. It was three in the afternoon before she found out that her daughter had been missing all day. Then she rang the police.

PC Boote was panicking.

As soon as the report of a missing girl came through, he realised that this was the very same girl he had seen that afternoon.

"And what happened to her, police constable?" asked the station sergeant.

"She walked out of the station, sarge," mumbled PC Boote.

"And?"

"Er, I think I might have seen her walking off with a tramp."

The police sergeant sighed and reached for a telephone. This could be serious – very serious indeed.

"But I don't understand why you're all dressed in rags, Ms Wiz."

Lizzie and the tramp woman were sitting in a dingy café, drinking tea. Outside, it was already getting dark. An old man at the next table was darting suspicious looks in their direction as he shook a tomato ketchup bottle over his egg and chips.

"The last time I saw you," Lizzie continued, "you were a teacher."

Ms Wiz smiled.

"Do you remember what I told you then?" she asked. "I said I'd be back whenever a spot of magic was needed. So here I am."

"I see," said Lizzie quietly. She was beginning to wonder whether she was right to be here, sitting in a café with Ms Wiz. A worrying thought had occurred to her. Maybe it was somebody *pretending* to be Ms Wiz. What if this was the Danger Stranger she had always been told never to talk to?

"Watch," said the tramp woman, as if she could read Lizzie's mind.

There was a low hum from where she was sitting.

"Blimey!" said the man sitting at

the next-door table as the contents of
the tomato ketchup bottle covered
his plate.

"That's not magic," said Lizzie.
"That's life."

There was a slurping noise as the
ketchup disappeared back into the
bottle.

"*Blimey*!" gasped the man.

"Ms Wiz!" said Lizzie, laughing for
the first time that day. "You never
change, do you?"

"Only in the way I look," said Ms Wiz, taking a notebook from her pocket. "Now let's get down to business."

"D'you want a pen?" asked Lizzie.

"That won't be necessary," said Ms Wiz. "Cat's name?"

"Waif."

"Missing for how long?"

"Two days."

"Distinguishing features?"

"Green eyes, lovely white coat with

ginger patches . . ." Lizzie sighed as she remembered Waif. "Very friendly."

"Other facts known?"

"Only that everyone round here seems to have lost a cat."

"Mmm." Ms Wiz looked thoughtful. "Seems a strange coincidence."

"Yes," said Lizzie. "It is strange and all the lost cat notices mentioned that they had nice coats. That seemed a bit odd."

"Odd," said Ms Wiz, "and worrying. It's time for us to get moving."

"Aren't you going to note anything down?" asked Lizzie.

"Whoops, silly me," said Ms Wiz, staring hard at the notebook. As if an invisible hand were writing, the page quickly filled up with notes. "There you go," she said briskly.

Lizzie shook her head. Nothing was ever straightforward when Ms Wiz was around. "Now what do we do?" she asked.

"I'm going to tell you our plan," said Ms Wiz. "But before that, we're going to write to your mother, who'll be worrying about you. Then we're going home."

"To *your* home?" Lizzie couldn't believe her ears. When she was a teacher, Ms Wiz had always been very mysterious about where she lived and no one from Class Five had been invited back.

"It's not much," shrugged Ms Wiz, "but I think you'll like it."

It was dark by the time a letter from Lizzie was slipped under Mrs Thompson's door.

It read:

Dear Mum

Please don't worry about me. I'm alright and I've met up with someone who's going to use magic to help me find Waif.

Do you remember Ms Wiz, our magical teacher? People called her a witch but she always said that she was a Paranormal operative. Well, it's her. Except now she's a tramp.

I'm staying at Ms Wiz's home so everything is alright.

Love

Lizzie
xxx

PS Don't get the police to look for us. They probably wouldn't recognize me since Ms Wiz's plan is to turn me into a cat!!!

Mrs Thompson read the note again. Slowly the awful truth began to sink in.

Her only daughter had run off with a tramp ...

Or maybe a witch ...

And she was about to be turned into a cat ... !

With a little cry, Mrs Thompson ran to telephone the police.

CHAPTER THREE
MAGIC – OR TROUBLE?

"Is this it?"

Lizzie was unable to keep the disappointment from her voice when they reached Ms Wiz's home.

Because it wasn't really a home at all. It was an extremely old car with flat tyres and dents all over it. It did have curtains but even they were more like rags, hung over the windows to stop people peering in.

"Yes, this is it," said Ms Wiz proudly. "What d'you think?"

"Interesting," said Lizzie, who didn't want to hurt Ms Wiz's feelings. "Not quite what I expected but . . . interesting."

"If you like it now, just wait until you step inside."

Ms Wiz opened the door with a flourish. Lizzie gasped.

From the outside, Ms Wiz's car had looked no more than a tangle of rusty, useless metal, just the sort of place where you might expect a tramp to live, but inside . . .

. . . it was even worse. All that Lizzie could see were torn, grey rugs, old newspapers and half-eaten sandwiches. Then something moved on the back seat – something small and grey.

"A rat!" Lizzie screamed.

"Of course," said Ms Wiz. "Don't you remember Herbert, my magic rat?"

She picked up Herbert and clambered into the car. "You can use the guest bedroom," she said, pointing to the back seat. Reluctantly, Lizzie climbed in.

"Close the door behind you," said Ms Wiz.

Something very strange happened as Lizzie pulled the door shut. There was a low hum and, as if someone had thrown a switch somewhere, the car started changing. The front seats turned around and became small armchairs. A table with crisps and lemonade appeared out of the floor. The back seat became a sofa. And the gearstick was transformed into a lamp which lit up the inside of the car with a soft pink glow.

Lizzie couldn't believe her eyes. It was as if she was no longer in a rusty old wreck of a car but in a warm country cottage.

"Being a paranormal operative has its advantages," smiled Ms Wiz.

"What are we going to do now?" asked Lizzie, settling down on the sofa. She was beginning to feel sleepy.

"We'll wait up for the catnappers," said Ms Wiz.

"Catnappers?"

"That's where your Waif has gone," said Ms Wiz. "And those other cats. They've been kidnapped, I'm sure of it."

"But why?"

"Gloves," said Ms Wiz grimly. "Fur gloves. That's why all the cats that have disappeared have nice coats."

Suddenly Lizzie felt afraid. Looking under bushes was one thing. But staying up all night to catch a

gang of catnappers? For a moment, she wished she was back in her bed, safe.

"Help yourself to crisps," said Ms Wiz, peering through the curtains into the darkness of the park outside. "I'll keep look-out. All the local cats come to this park at night and I have a feeling that our friends the catnappers will be here too. They'll lead us to Waif."

"How do you know he's alive?" Lizzie asked.

"Let's just put it down to intuition," said Ms Wiz.

Lizzie felt braver now. After all, she was with Ms Wiz. They had magic on their side.

"Jack, a policeman's here to ask you some questions."

Jack Beddows had just been dozing off when his mother switched on the light. There, in his bedroom, stood a policeman with a notebook in his hand.

"Sorry to interrupt your beauty sleep, young man," said PC Boote, "but we have a small emergency concerning your friend Lizzie."

Jack rubbed his eyes. "What's happened to her?" he asked.

"Her mother has received a letter

which gives us reason to believe
that she has been abducted by a
certain—" PC Boote looked in his
notebook "—Ms Wiz."

"Ms Wiz!" Jack sat up in his bed.
"Where is she?"

"That's the problem," said PC
Boote. "At first we thought she was
just a tramp but now it turns out that
she's an all-round troublemaker. We
think Lizzie's gone off with her."

"That's all right then," said Jack.

"All right?" PC Boote seemed surprised. "According to information received, this Ms Wiz has in the past turned teachers into geese, removed a school inspector's trousers and released about a thousand white mice into the children's ward of a general hospital. That's not what I call all right."

"Ms Wiz is magic," said Jack.

PC Boote put on his most serious expression. "You call it magic, son," he said "I call it trouble. Now, we need to know exactly what she looks like."

"Here we go," said Ms Wiz, peering through the curtains of her car.

A van drew up by the gates of the park. Two men in dark clothes stepped out and climbed over the railings. The younger and taller of the two men was carrying a net while the other, a short, elderly man with a slight limp, followed him, whistling softly.

"Come on then," whispered Ms Wiz, shaking Lizzie by the shoulder.

"Mmmm?" said Lizzie sleepily.

"Our friends are here," said Ms Wiz. "It's time to put our plan into action."

After no more than half an hour, the men returned. They were carrying two cats, trapped in the net.

"This tabby puss is a young 'un," said the older man. "Shall I let it go?"

"Young or old, makes no difference," said the other man, opening the back of the van and bundling the cats into a sack. "And stop calling them 'puss'. Sometimes I think you're too soft for this game."

"What do we do now?" Lizzie

whispered as, moments later, the van began to move.

"Follow them, of course," answered Ms Wiz. "Just because my home's got four flat tyres, it doesn't mean it can't go."

And, sure enough, the old car seemed to raise itself slightly at that moment and, as if hovering just above the ground, moved quietly forward to follow the van.

"The moment we arrive, we put our plan into action," said Ms Wiz as they drove quietly down the dark streets, always keeping a safe distance from the catnappers in front of them.

"Right," said Lizzie quietly. She was thinking of her mother, and how worried she would be. Still, there was no going back now.

Ms Wiz glanced over her shoulder.

"Nervous?" she asked.

"Not really," Lizzie lied. "So long as you're there to help."

Soon the van drew up outside a large dark house with closed shutters.

"I know this place," whispered Lizzie. "It's called the Old Hospital."

"All right," said Ms Wiz, stopping the car. "Ready?"

The men were getting out and opening the back of the van.

"Ready," said Lizzie, closing her eyes.

There was a low hum from the front of the car. Lizzie felt as if she had been slapped hard on the back. When she opened her eyes, everything in the car was bigger. She was looking up at Ms Wiz, who was smiling.

"What a lovely cat," Ms Wiz said. "Now remember the plan. You follow them into the house and, as soon as you're alone with the cats, scratch your left ear three times. I'll be outside and, as soon as I get that message, I'll turn you back into Lizzie again. Then you let the cats out, all right?"

"Sure," said Lizzie with a cat smile. To her surprise, she found that she could still talk in her normal voice.

The men were carrying the sack up the steps to the house when Lizzie, now a sleek black cat, went after them.

As they opened the door, she slipped in behind them.

Ms Wiz stood by her car, staring up at the house. "Good luck, Lizzie," she muttered.

It was then that she felt a heavy hand on her shoulder.

"You're nicked, Ms Wiz," said PC Boote.

CHAPTER FOUR
ABANDONED

It wasn't bad being a cat, Lizzie discovered.

Nobody noticed you, for example. You could creep under tables and hide in the shadows. You could jump onto window-ledges, as if it were the most natural thing in the world. And, even if you did lose your balance, you always seemed to land on your feet. It was quite fun.

Or at least it would have been if Lizzie had been in a normal house rather than in a catnappers' den.

Lizzie quickly discovered where they kept the cats. The older of the catnappers had trudged down to the cellar with the sack on his back. There was an unearthly yowling sound as a door was opened.

"There you go, my lovelies," he said. "Good puss." Lizzie heard hissing and scrabbling as the two new cats were bundled into the room. She ducked under a chair as the man returned, carrying an empty sack.

"That's about it then," he said to the other catnapper. "Mrs D'Arcy from the fur shop will be along tomorrow morning to tell us which ones she needs. Then," – for a moment he looked almost sad – "It's bye-bye, pussies."

"This is the last time I take you on a job," said the younger man. "Honestly, a catnapper that likes cats! I've heard it all now."

The older man sniffed. "I feel sorry for them, that's all. You wouldn't understand."

"If you like them so much, you'd better feed them."

The man fetched a paper sack of cat food and calling out, "Din-dins, pussies," he limped down the stairs. Lizzie followed.

For a moment, as he opened the door and threw some food in, there was total confusion in the room – and, in that moment, Lizzie slipped in.

What she saw took her breath away.

There were cats everywhere. Some were fighting over the food, some were miaowing pitifully, some were pacing backwards and forwards, some were simply asleep. One or two of the cats, startled to hear a human voice coming from a cat, arched their backs and hissed nervously.

"Don't worry," said Lizzie, carefully stepping through the throng of cats. "I'm just looking for someone. I'm not really a cat myself."

At that moment, a big ginger tom stepped forward and cuffed her around the ear.

"Ow!" said Lizzie. Without thinking she tapped him back, leaving her claws out. Surprised, the tom retreated backwards into a tabby, which bit him.

"Stop fighting, you stupid animals," said Lizzie angrily. "Don't you realise that tomorrow you could be . . ." At that moment, Lizzie saw a familiar white form in a corner. "Waif?"

The white cat stirred, recognising the voice, and gave a soft miaow. Lizzie looked closer. Yes it *was* Waif – asleep as usual.

It was time for action. Soon the catnappers would be going to bed. All Lizzie needed to do was to give Ms Wiz the signal to turn her back into a human, sneak out of the door, and then lead the cats to freedom.

Bracing herself for the shock, Lizzie scratched herself three times behind the left ear.

Nothing happened.

"Come on, Ms Wiz," she muttered, trying to keep calm. "Get that magic working." She scratched again, harder this time.

But nothing happened.

"Ms Wiz, where *are* you?" With growing desperation, Lizzie scratched and scratched and scratched.

But absolutely nothing happened.

"Don't you understand? Magic doesn't work at long distance. I can't change Lizzie back into a little girl from here."

Ms Wiz was sitting in a small, white-walled room at the police station. For the past hour, she had been trying to explain to PC Boote exactly why she needed to return to the catnappers' house as soon as possible.

"I see," said the police constable. "So your, er, magic is a bit like my walkie-talkie, is it? You have to be in range for it to work."

Ms Wiz sighed wearily. Why was it that grown-ups found it so difficult to understand magic when children found it so easy?

"That's right," she said.

"And you expect me to believe that you've cast a spell—" PC Boote could hardly keep the disbelief out of his voice "—transforming Lizzie Thompson into a cat in order to save a load of moggies from a couple of nasty men who want to turn them into gloves. And that's why you were at the Old Hospital."

"Precisely," said Ms Wiz.

"You must think I'm daft."

Ms Wiz was about to reply when the door opened. It was the station sergeant.

"Any luck, constable?" he asked.

"I'm afraid not," said PC Boote. "We're still in the land of witches and wizards."

"Right," said the sergeant. "She can spend the night in the cells. Tomorrow morning we've got two of Lizzie's classmates coming in to tell us whether this really is the famous Ms Wiz."

"You don't seem to understand," said Ms Wiz. "Tomorrow could be too late."

PC Boote turned to the sergeant and, with a grim little smile, tapped the side of his head.

At first, when they were led into the small room at the police station, Jack

and Caroline didn't recognise Ms Wiz. After a worried, sleepless night in the cells, she looked more like a tired, dishevelled tramp than ever.

Then she smiled.

"Ms Wiz!" said Caroline, hugging her.

"You look so different," said Jack.

"Hullo, Caroline and Jack," said Ms Wiz. "Could you explain to this policeman who I am?"

But, as the children told PC Boote about Ms Wiz, he continued to look suspicious.

"I'll need to discuss this with my superiors," he said eventually.

"There's no time for that," said Ms Wiz angrily. She turned to the children. "Do either of you know the way to the Old Hospital?"

"I do," said Jack.

Suddenly the sound of a low hum

filled the room. PC Boote was just about to speak when something very odd happened. He turned into a white rabbit.

"Sorry about that," said Ms Wiz, unlocking the door to the room with the keys that were now on the floor. "Let's go, children."

The police station now appeared to be completely empty, except for a number of white rabbits.

"Did you have to turn the whole police force into rabbits?" asked Jack as they hurried out of the main entrance. "There's going to be terrible trouble."

"I couldn't mess around," said Ms Wiz briskly. "This is a matter of life and death."

"Why didn't you do it earlier then?" asked Caroline.

"I didn't know the way to the Old Hospital," said Ms Wiz. "I may be magic but my sense of direction is terrible."

Outside the station stood a police car. Ms Wiz opened the car door and, pushing a white rabbit aside, leapt into the driver's seat.

"Jump in!" she shouted. The police car's engine started with a roar. "Let's just hope we're in time."

CHAPTER FIVE
FUR FREE

A thin ray of light penetrated the gloom of the cellar at the Old Hospital. Lizzie lay dozing, curled up beside Waif. Her left ear was sore from where she had been scratching all night. She was frightened.

Some of the cats around her stirred restlessly as they heard the sound of footsteps approaching the cellar. The door was flung open to reveal the most extraordinary woman Lizzie had ever seen. She was very tall and was wearing fur from head to foot.

"Ugh, disgusting!" said the woman. "If there's one thing I hate, it's live creatures."

"Think of them as pelts, Mrs D'Arcy," said the younger catnapper

nervously. "That's what they will be soon."

Mrs D'Arcy looked around the room.

"Frankly," she said, "there are some pelts here that I wouldn't allow my chauffeur to clean my car with."

The older man looked shocked. "Madam uses fur on her car?" he asked.

"I use fur for everything," said Mrs D'Arcy with a dangerous smile.

"Every item of clothing that I wear was once alive." She stroked her soft mink coat. "Now – let's get down to business. Count these horrible animals and I'll tell you how much I can pay."

The police car arrived at the Old Hospital with a squeal of brakes.

"Look, Ms Wiz!" said Jack, pointing to a large grey Rolls Royce, with a number plate which read "FUR 1", which was parked outside the front door.

"Just as I feared," said Ms Wiz, jumping out. "The fur merchant is here. Come on!"

Jack and Caroline followed her up the steps. Without hesitating, Ms Wiz kicked the front door, causing it to open with a loud crack.

"Wow," said Caroline. "Magic!"

"No," said Ms Wiz grimly. "That wasn't magic. That was anger."

Just then the older catnapper limped up the stairs from the cellar.

" 'Ere, what are you lot doing?" he said.

"We're here for the cats, so don't try and stop us," said Ms Wiz.

The old man smiled. "Stop you rescuing my little pussies? Why would I do that?" He winked as he walked past them towards the door. "I'll leave you to it. Good luck."

"Was *that* magic?" asked Jack.

"No, I think it was something called conscience," replied Ms Wiz.

At that moment, the three of them became aware of someone else climbing the stairs towards them.

"I don't know who you are," said a loud voice from the darkness in front of them. "But my name is Mrs D'Arcy. I'm very rich, very powerful and, when I'm annoyed, I can be very unpleasant."

"Careful, Ms Wiz," whispered Jack. "She looks as if she means it."

"We want those cats," Ms Wiz called out. "Open that door right now."

Mrs D'Arcy laughed. "I'm sure you do," she said. "From the way you're dressed, you look as if you could use a fur coat."

"I'm fur free," said Ms Wiz, moving closer.

"That's quite far enough," warned Mrs D'Arcy. "You're probably absolutely filthy. I don't want any nasty marks on my fur coat."

"What fur coat?" asked Ms Wiz innocently, as the sound of a low hum filled the basement stairs.

Automatically, Mrs D'Arcy touched her coat – and gasped. The fur was beginning to move, as if it had a life of its own.

"What's happening?" she said, going pale.

"Nothing much," said Ms Wiz. "I'll release the cats in a moment. But first of all, I want to free the animals that made your coat."

Before Jack's and Caroline's astonished eyes, Mrs D'Arcy's clothes were becoming a writhing mass of animals.

"But everything I'm wearing is fur," she shrieked.

"Oh dear," said Ms Wiz. "How very embarrassing."

By now, Mrs D'Arcy's coat had completely disappeared and several small, furry animals were shaking and scratching themselves at her feet. With a scream, she ran up the stairs, as the rest of her clothes began to turn back into animals.

Ms Wiz opened the door to the cellar. The second of the two catnappers was standing, apparently unable to move, in the middle of the room. One of the cats had gone to sleep on his feet.

"I thought of turning him into a mouse," said Ms Wiz. "But in the end I decided on a human statue. Cats can be so cruel."

"There's Waif!" shouted Caroline, pointing across the room.

"Never mind Waif," said Jack. "What about Lizzie?"

At that moment, a sleek black cat stretched sleepily and scratched herself three times behind the left ear.

"Lizzie!"

Within moments of becoming a human being again, Lizzie had telephoned her mother. Now, minutes

later, mother and daughter were
hugging each other joyfully on the
steps of the Old Hospital.

"Where's Waif?" asked Mrs
Thompson.

"He's being fed in the kitchen with
the other cats," said Jack. "We're
going to hold on to them until we can
find all their owners."

"And who on earth is that odd
woman hiding in the Rolls Royce
without any clothes on?"

Lizzie laughed. "It's a long
story," she said. "Perhaps Ms Wiz had
better explain it. Where is she, by the
way?"

"Oh no!" said Jack, who had
noticed Ms Wiz's battered old car
rising slowly off its flat tyres like a
hovercraft about to move off. "She
can't go now."

A white rabbit was hopping busily
down the road towards them.

"Ms Wiz!" shouted Lizzie. "You've forgotten the police! They're still rabbits!"

The car hesitated and hovered with a low hum.

"All right," said PC Boote, shaking himself as if he had just awoken from a rather strange dream. "Where are these catnappers then?"

"The ringleader's over there," said Lizzie, pointing to Mrs D'Arcy's car. "But she's—"

"No buts," said the policeman. "Leave this to me."

He walked slowly towards the Rolls Royce.

"Right, you in there," he said, bending down to look in the window. "You're nicked. Er, you're nacked. Oh no, you're absolutely n-n-n-naked!"

He turned away, blushing.

And everyone, even PC Boote, started laughing.